I0520028

Less Than Yesterday

Lilith Jones

HOT ROMANCE EROTICA

WARNING

This book contains sexually explicit scenes and adult language. It may be considered offensive to some readers. This book is for sale to adults ONLY.

* * * * * * * * * * * * * * * * * *

Please store your files wisely where they cannot be accessed by underage readers.

Please feel free to send me an email. Just know that these emails are filtered by my publisher. Good news is always welcome.

About the Publisher

4Fun Publishing, a member of **BLVNP Incorporated**, 340 S. Lemon #6200, Walnut CA 91789, info@blvnp.com / legal@blvnp.com
NOTE: Due to the highly emotional reaction of some people to works of erotic fiction, any email sent to the above address that contains foul language or religious references is automatically deleted by our anti-spam software and will not be seen. All other communications are welcome.

DISCLAIMER

Please don't be stupid and kill yourself. This book is a work of FICTION. Do not try any new sexual practice that you find in this book. It is fiction and not to be confused with reality. Neither the author nor the publisher or its associates assume any responsibility for any loss, injury, death or legal consequences resulting from acting on the contents in this book. Every character in this book is over 18 years of age. The author's opinions are not to be construed as the opinions of the publisher. The material in this book is for entertainment purposes ONLY. Enjoy.

Less Then Yesterday
Hot Romance Erotica

By: Lilith Jones

© **Lilith Jones 2015**
ISBN: 978-1-68030-293-6

Jess was looking for the second earring of the pair she wanted to wear to dinner, and the box was a mess. Scrabbling through the tangled chains and too-young costume jewelry, she came upon the necklace that Ted had given her years before. It had once been a favorite, but she hasn't worn it for a year.

"*Plus que hier — moins que demain,*" it said. "More than yesterday, less than tomorrow."

When he'd given it to her, sophomore year, Ted had probably intended it to communicate how his love for her was growing. She'd worn it to describe how her love for him grew. Now, she shoved it into a back corner and finally found the earring. When she held up the string of pearls which went with those earrings, Ted came up behind her to fasten them around her neck. After six years of knowing him — three of them married years — she still marveled how those large hands, which looked so rough and clumsy, were really so gentle and dexterous.

"You clean up well," she said when she'd risen and looked at him. In his sports coat, Ted's 6' 5", broad-shouldered frame looked impressive. The geek glasses softened his rugged-looking face. From their first date, she had liked having a guy who towered over her 5' 9". He still made her feel dainty.

If her feelings for him had changed, she mused going down the stairs, it sure wasn't that he looked less attractive. It wasn't fair. Her prettiness was fading with time, and he was starting to look mature.

Sitting beside Ted in the car on the way to the dinner, she reflected that she hadn't really fallen out of love with him. It wasn't that he beat her or anything. Ted was nice, and she loved him. It was just that Ted-2014 was much less exciting than Ted-2011 had been. Well, Ted-2011 wasn't available. Even if he were — even if she could get in a time machine and leave her present husband for the man she loved more — he would age into a duller man over the next three years.

Though she was bored for the next four hours, she could hardly blame Ted for that. Her boss, Dave Anderson, was one of a dozen people being honored by the Realtors' Association at the dinner. She and Ted were both bored, and — even if he was looking at his cell an embarrassing number of times — Ted was attending the dinner for her.

Finally, Dave got up to receive his award. His speech, maybe because she'd written it, sounded better to her than his predecessors' speeches. Ted must have thought so, too.

"Three minutes, eight seconds," he said. "That's the first of the three-minute speeches that clocked in at under four minutes, only the third under five. P.O.E.M. strikes again."

That she was a card-carrying member of the Professional Organization of English Majors was one of their family jokes. The guy up after Dave hadn't had a good speech writer; she couldn't tell whether he'd even prepared anything. It felt like three minutes when he finished his introductory joke. She went back to musing.

The honeymoon was definitely over. Their first year of marriage had been sexy. They had both worked, but when they got out, they came together.

They'd met in college, she from Denver and he from Kansas. Neither had known anyone in San Francisco, but his programming degree was worth more there. The first summer, not knowing people was a bonus. They'd spent week-end days exploring San Francisco and nights exploring each other. Not that Ted kept his hands off her on the cable cars. Not that they didn't spend the occasional Saturday without leaving the apartment. She could remember two Saturdays when they hadn't even dressed.

They had gradually made friends: her coworkers, his coworkers, other couples in the first neighborhood, other U of Colorado graduates in the SF area. Now, there were enough friends that they seldom spent either a Friday or a Saturday night by themselves. Even when they were home, they were likelier to be entertaining than spending the day in pajamas. They'd lived in the present apartment for more than a year and had yet to eat lunch there nude.

Applause broke out around her. The latest speaker must have finished at last. She joined in. "Eight minutes," Ted said. The letter to Dave had said that acceptance speeches were to be no longer than three minutes.

"Well," Ted said on the drive home, "you could bring in some bucks as a speech writer. I'm sure that Dave would give you a recommendation."

"Do we really need more money?" She'd been thinking that the two of them didn't have enough time together, and Ted had been thinking that she needed to work more hours. To be fair to him, he put in extra time at work and made one hell of a lot more than she did. Still . . .

"More? Hell, not now! I was thinking about your working at home after you have a baby. It would be a lot easier than going back to work."

"We said we wouldn't start a baby until we'd gone for a year without needing my paycheck," she said. It hadn't been a year, had it?

"Well, I wasn't talking about starting anything tonight. It's been more than eleven months. And, if we aren't going to make the goal next month, where is the huge expenditure going to come from? . . . Not to end a sentence with a preposition or anything."

"Ted! That's not really a rule."

"Yes, dear," Ted said, sounding like he thought she was trying to change the subject. He was probably right, too, but he didn't pursue the subject. Ted was, she kept reminding herself, nice.

Thursday, a few weeks later, she started a new disk of pills. That night, with Ted working late, she realized what that meant. If she did what they had agreed, it would be her last disk of pills for a good, long while. She thought for a minute about keeping them from meeting the conditions by dipping into her savings to buy a new, costly wardrobe. The account was in her name, after all; she needn't consult Ted. Really, though, she could delay the pregnancy more sensibly than that. She could tell him that she wanted to wait longer before they had a baby.

Then, though, she would have to tell him why. Even if she trashed her savings account, he would ask why. She did not want to answer. You could tell a guy you didn't love him anymore; you couldn't tell him that you still loved him — but you loved him less. You certainly couldn't tell him that you were afraid to have a baby with him because you were afraid that you'd love him even less in five or ten years.

And she did want babies. She had been an only child of a single mother, and she wanted four. Ted, who had been the third of four, had warned her that she was romanticizing the experience. "Sure, I want kids. We'll have one, and we can decide about the next after we have some experience with that one."

That sure didn't leave her much wiggle room now. She wanted kids; she wanted Ted's kids. They might inherit his brains, and he would be a patient father. She wanted his kids, and she wanted to raise them with him. She just wasn't sure she wanted to be with him for another eighteen years to do the job.

But, if not Ted, who? She still loved Ted. Thinking that she might someday love him so little that she might want to leave him was no reason to leave him now.

Of course, single women had children every day. So leaving Ted wasn't deciding not to ever have kids. That was stupid, though. She was afraid of having a baby now because she was afraid of raising it as a single mother. She certainly didn't want to leave Ted — merely feared that she would want to sometime in the future.

By the time that Ted got home, she was eager to see him, so eager that she was already in a sexy nightie.

"Have dinner?" she asked.

"Yeah. I brought you some left-overs if you want them for lunch tomorrow." She carried lunch; his cafeteria was so heavily subsidized that buying lunch at work was cheaper for him than brown-bagging it. Dinner after seven was free. Nothing was too good for programmers who stayed late. "Is it too late?" For sex, he meant.

"I adore Theodore." And, really, she still did. She hadn't used that silly couplet for a while, but it still applied.

"Well, I adore Jessica, too. Give me a few minutes, and I'll prove it." While he was in the bathroom, she took off the nightie. Then she got into bed and pulled the sheet up to her neck.

Ted got into bed without baring an inch of her. Then he leaned over and kissed her before resting on one elbow and slowly drawing the sheet off her.

"It must be Christmas. Santa brought me what I've always wanted." He kissed her again. Then his mouth trailed down to her right breast. His chin scratched, but the scratches were exciting. When his tongue and lips on her nipple had aroused her, she spread her legs. He stroked her cleft until she tensed.

"Ted."

"Yes." He moved over her and between her knees, which she raised. Then he opened her, filled her. "Jess." His chest hair tickled her nipples as he moved above her and inside her. She licked salt from where his neck joined his shoulder. Her arousal gyred upward with each of his strokes. The tension broke, and she thrust herself at him and around him.

"Jess," he said as she clutched around him. "Sssi," as he drove her into the mattress. "Cah!" as he throbbed within her contractions. He collapsed on her, and they gasped into each other's' ears.

Somewhat later, he pulled himself off and lay on his side inches away. When she backed into him, he wrapped himself around her.

"You are," he whispered, "the sexiest woman in the whole world." They fell asleep in the spoon, although they woke on their own sides these days. She put the nightgown on and covered it with a bathrobe before cooking breakfast. They kissed lightly before going out the door on their separate ways to their separate work.

It wasn't that Ted ignored her satisfaction, she mused on the commute. He took care to bring her to climax every time. It was just that he brought her to climax in almost the same way almost every time. Ted was a considerate lover — just as he was considerate about doing his share of the housework and letting her choose her share of their TV shows and her share of their entertainment and socializing. Ted was nice. Was nice enough?

Maybe the dullness — relative dullness — of their current life was partly her fault. What if she greeted him when he got in from his next late night in harem pants with belly-dance music on in the entertainment center? Of course, while he warned her when he had to stay late, he didn't tell her how late he would be. She didn't want to spend the night in harem pants and have him stumble in at midnight unable to function.

Friday, weeks later, Ted asked out of the blue, "This was payday, wasn't it?" Her pay was on direct deposit, and they had shifted the deposit to her savings account. Nothing came to his notice, and damned little to her notice, when the checks went in. He could figure it out, but why had he bothered?

"Yeah."

"It was the twenty-seventh paycheck; you haven't touched that money. We now know that we can live on my paycheck alone."

"I took the money out and lost it gambling on molybdenum futures," she said.

"Yeah, right! You having second thoughts?"

"Well, it's a big step. I'm in the middle of my pills."

"When does this dispenser run out?" he asked.

"A week from Wednesday." Of course, the last seven weren't all that important.

"Then let's call two weeks from tomorrow F day. After that, we'll assume you're fertile. Do we have anything scheduled for that day?" He got up and went to the UNICEF calendar hanging on the kitchen wall that they used for recording social events. "Well, we do now." She could see him scratch a big X across the box, taking the entire day.

"I'm not sure, Ted," she said.

"Not sure about what?"

"Well, I'm not sure about anything." That was accurate. By now, she wasn't even sure about their marriage.

"Well, have you changed your mind about wanting kids?" Ted asked.

"Not really, but having kids now is a hell of a lot scarier than having kids someday."

"And," he said, "the only thing that's certain is that it won't be for nine months — leaving aside that it might not take."

"That's all so true." So true and so beside the point of her worries.

"Well, whatever our chances, we'd be idiots to go off the pill if you don't want children."

"We did decide," she said. Did she want to put it off? Did she want Ted to insist so that it was his decision and not hers? Would he suspect that she was dubious about them, about him? Well, nobody had ever accused Ted of being sensitive.

"That we did, but it's your body, and you can change your decision." Ted kept reminding her that whatever his faults, he was a nice guy. "If not now, though, when?"

That was a damned good question. When she was surer of him? When she was surer of her feelings about him? But if she felt this way after three years, she would never be able to be sure — really, rationally sure — in the foreseeable future. If her love increased, she would fear that it could decrease again someday.

And she just couldn't tell him how she felt. Having kids was scary, but telling him she was falling out of love with him was scarier.

"No!" she said suddenly. "Let's do it. I just had an attack of nerves." It had been more than an attack of nerves, or the nerves were about something else.

"Why molybdenum?"

"Huh?"

"When you told that stretcher about speculating, why in molybdenum, for God's sake?" Ted asked. "Why not in hogs' bellies?"

"That sounds gross. Molybdenum sounds exotic."

"You're cute. Molybdenum isn't exotic; it's a standard alloy in steel."

And, with his thinking that she was endearingly ignorant and her thinking that he was nice if not exciting, they went to bed and had enthusiastic sex. It was still safe sex, though.

She was committed, even so, and when she threw away the empty pill disk, she put the three remaining disks into a back corner of the shelf in the closet. Ted didn't say any more, but the black X on the calendar kept catching her eye.

Friday, Ted came back late, but not all that late. "I love you," he said. Then, when they were getting ready for bed, "Turn off the alarm, will you? We should sleep late." Still, he put on his pajamas before coming to bed, a sure sign that he didn't intend to make love that night. He acted loving — kissing her and cuddling her — but he didn't go any further.

In the morning, her bladder woke her later than the alarm would have. "Let me in as soon as you're finished," Ted said as she rushed to the bathroom. Instead of showering and putting on her face, she simply used the toilet and washed her hands before giving him his turn.

Ted, though, took his time. She could hear the shower running, while she lay in bed steaming over his making her delay her shower so he could take his. That wasn't really fair. Ted was almost always considerate, and it wasn't as though she would be late for an appointment. Still, she was getting tired of being fair; why wasn't Ted worrying about his being fair to her? When he came out he was shaven and had a towel wrapped around his waist.

"I'll finish up now," she said.

"No. Stay there," Ted said. "You can bathe later. What's the rush? What needs to be done today?"

"Well, breakfast for one thing."

"Bathe later and I'll fix breakfast." She gave him a look. His idea of fixing breakfast was pouring cereal into a bowl. "Well, brunch then. We have something scheduled for today, and it would be hard to accomplish outside."

He was really planning to celebrate what he'd called "F Day." When she'd asked, he claimed it stood for "fertility." He tossed the top sheet towards the foot of the bed. When he stripped off the towel she could see that he was more than half erect. The mattress jumped when he dropped onto the bed, and shifted again when he leaned over to kiss her. She could taste the toothpaste.

"If you hadn't rushed me," she said, "I would have brushed my teeth."

"I like your taste. I like your smell. I like your feel. I like you. I'd like more of you even more. Want to lose this?" He was tugging at her nightie.

She helped him remove it. This time, when he kissed her, his hand wandered over her in interesting ways. Her arousal had started later than his, but it was coming right along now. If he waited a little, and Ted almost always waited long enough, she could join him in his climax.

When he kissed down to her right breast, the smooth chin gave his progress an unusual feel. His hand smoothed down to her mound. She spread her legs, but he got lost in kissing circles around her breast and playing with her pubic hair. She felt the heat rising in her, but she needed more. She finally took his hand and pushed it between her legs.

"Smooth," he said, "silky smooth." Then, he licked her nipple and stroked over her clit at the same time. Fire shot through her. He sucked the nipple at the same time he took long strokes between her labia. Every time he got to the clit, he tongued the nipple again. Heat built in her groin. She could feel herself getting close. Still, he made no move to come in. Her body tensed. This time, she would be ahead of him.

"Ted," she warned him.

"Yes, darling. I know. Let it come to you. Come for me." Having raised himself to say that, he switched nipples. She felt his chest hair scratch her sensitized right nipple as he sucked and tongued her left one. With that encouragement, with that loving, with the sum of all his stimulating touches, she was about to go over.

The fire blazed. With only a hand and a mouth holding her to the mattress, she writhed.

"Imm hmm," he said around her nipple. The strokes continued; the fire blazed again. Then it blazed a third time, hotter than ever.

When she relaxed, he stilled his hand and kissed her forehead. "You are so beautiful," he said. He kissed her nose tip and her chin. Then he lay down beside her with his arm across her waist. As her breathing eased, he kissed her shoulder occasionally.

"I'm not really beautiful," she corrected him. She was losing even the fresh prettiness she had had when she'd met him. If he lied about beauty, which she could check in the mirror, how was she to believe him when he said he loved her?

"You're always lovely. You're lovelier like that. I could put a mirror in the ceiling so you could look."

"No." Aside from the bedroom being where their friends left their coats, the landlord's having to see it sometimes, and the fear of the mirror falling on her at a critical moment, she didn't want to see herself in the midst of sex. Voyeurism was his fetish, not hers.

"Well," he said, "you're arguing about something you won't check. You ready for the next phase?"

"Sure. This was a strange way to utilize my fertility." Not that she was likely to be fertile yet.

"Well, before something will grow in your garden, I have to till it a little bit first."

"Is that what I am?" she asked. "Your garden?"

"It is your garden, my sweet, and a very sweet garden it is. I'm just the gardener who's going to do the planting." He started, though, on her lips. The sensations from present mild caresses mixed with the anticipation of promised future deep ones to arouse her. She could feel her nipples and labia swell before his lips and hands reached them. When he reached her more sensitive parts, the strokes of fingers and tongue soothed her need. They aroused deeper needs, though.

"Oh," she said when he stroked across her clit and sucked her nipple simultaneously. The heat spread to her fingers and toes. As he stroked her and sucked her, her thighs grew too hot. She spread them to let the heat escape, especially the heat where they met. He climbed between them, never removing his finger. Well, at last! She was ready for him — would probably come before he did.

When he was in position, though, he squatted between her knees and put his mouth where she had been expecting his cock.

"Ted?" When was he going to start his planting? Then the sensations were too intense to let her express any questions. She was moaning, but not saying any words.

Ted slipped his hands under her butt and raised her to his mouth. He licked her clit while squeezing her ass cheeks. She trembled on that unsteady platform, and pushed down with both hands and feet to steady herself. The heat consumed her, and she pushed upwards into his mouth. When he sucked, the fire burst in her. Wave after wave flared through her. She writhed and fell to her side.

He stopped sucking and licking, but he did kiss her thigh as she lay panting.

"I should have showered," she said when she'd got her breath back.

"I like your taste. I particularly like your smell." He came up in the bed beside her. "You are one sexy woman." He pulled her hand to his lips and began to kiss her fingers. As he sucked each finger, the warmth and wetness of his mouth and the smoothness of his tongue started her back on the road to arousal. His hand stroked her vulva, and she could feel the finger smoothing along the fringe of her labia, getting nearer and nearer to her clit, and then retreating. The heat built yet again.

"This time, you," she said reaching for him.

"Mmm! I thought you'd never ask." He moved over her while she kept her legs sprawled and against the mattress.

As a matter of fact, she *had* asked earlier. Still, she was even more eager now. She raised her knees when he was safely between them and spread herself while he supported his weight with one arm and brought his cock to her entrance with the other.

"So warm," he said when he was barely within. "So wet," as he was filling her. "So welcoming," when he filled her while his mound mashed against hers and his body stretched over her. He rested fully on her and in her with the top of his chest warming her cheek and his chin against her hairline. He adjusted his position so his weight was on his elbows and his hands were on her breasts. She raised her head to kiss his collarbone.

He slid his thumbs up her nipples before beginning long, slow strokes. She held his buttocks, appreciating the flexing muscles driving him in and out, appreciating the slide of his cock as the head spread her entrance going in and then the shaft stroked her there, appreciating the pressure against her when he was deepest, appreciating the shaft rubbing her again on the way out.

"I love you, you know," he said.

"You too." And she did love him, like this probably more than any other time. She felt herself tense, and she began to thrust back into his thrusts.

"Jess," he said. His butt tensed, but he maintained his pace. She pushed up more strongly, and pulled him against her by his butt when their loins met.

The fire shot through her, and she felt herself clasp him deep within her.

"Oh, Jess!" He drove her down into the mattress, and she felt him throb within her clasp. His butt was rock-hard within her hands. Then he was all soft except the pelvic bones which were digging into her thighs. When her thighs dropped, he slipped down between them. He and she lay breathing out of rhythm for a long time.

When he stirred, it was to move to her side. He left only one arm draped over her ribs under her breasts. Minutes later, he kissed her shoulder.

"I should take that shower, now," she said. She must be even more fragrant after this.

"Lie here; let it soak in a little more. I'll draw you a bath."

"Why thank you," she said. 'Letting it soak in' wouldn't make her pregnant at this time in the month. She had taken her last real pill ten days ago. Still, his care for her was wonderful. Today, it was easy to remember why she loved Ted.

When she heard the water shut off and went in, she found that the bathroom was redolent of bath salts. She washed briefly and then lay back in the luxury. She was a busy woman with never enough time for what needed to be done. Having time to simply rest, especially with the recent memories to enjoy, was making the morning even more special.

"Milady's luncheon is served," Ted said from the doorway some time later. He was wearing khakis and an apron. She put the nightie, robe, and slippers back on. Coffee wasn't the only odor which greeted her when they got to the kitchen. "They had shrimp fried rice for lunch, and I bought home some left-overs. I thought I'd put it in some shrimp-flavor ramen to warm it up." He'd also sliced a tomato and cooked some lima beans.

It wasn't a combination that she would add to her menu choices, but it tasted remarkably good. I-didn't-have-to-cook improves the flavor of any meal. It was even sort of balanced: shrimp for meat, noodles and rice for starch, vegetable, and a salad. Ted was trying. He was **very** trying at times, but this wasn't one of those times.

"Delicious," she said when she was half-way through her second cup of coffee. "Back in college, I would have suspected that any man who treated me to such a fine meal was after something."

"Me? I'm perfectly innocent." He made a face to show how innocent. Innocent was not one of Ted's more persuasive looks.

"Oh, I believe you. Why don't you fill the dishwasher while I put on some clothes to go out?"

"Now, wait a minute," Ted said. "If I do the dishes after cooking the meal, then I *do* want something from you."

"I think we should take a break. I'm going to watch TV. When the dishwasher is loaded and the kitchen cleaned up, come join me in the living room." Watching TV together could be an occasion for cuddling without getting serious. They had been serious quite enough this morning.

"I think the bedroom is a more appropriate place for joining you." But she had years of experience ignoring his dirty jokes.

The TV gave her a choice among fishing, carpentry, and cartoons.

Ted came into the living room in just his trousers. Without speaking to her, he got out his laptop and began to browse. What had happened to his plans for today? Why was she watching cartoons if he wasn't going to sit beside her? When the ad came on, she turned the set off by the remote.

"Shall I compare thee to a summer day?" Ted began. He'd looked up a selection of love poems. Ted wasn't the most skilled reader of verse, but the thought was endearing.

After the third, she went to the bookshelf. Love was all very well, but he'd set aside this day for sex, not love. She read him "She Being Brand New" from one of her old college books.

"I knew I'd chosen the wrong major," he said when she'd finished.

"No. One of us has to make a living. You just don't have the right books. Here, read this." It was *Borne on the Blue Aegean*.

They adjourned to the bedroom with two books. She took off her robe, but kept her nightie. He took off his trousers but kept his boxers. They alternated, one sitting on the bed reading and the other lying down listening. Those poems had been mildly embarrassing in the cold light of the classroom. They were much more arousing when read by a half-naked man who ogled her half-naked self when it was her turn to read.

"Those are all I can think of right now," she said. "Want me to look in other books?"

"Nah! Brilliant idea, though. When I was a teen looking for the dirty parts of books, I never thought of poetry books."

"You started your career as a dirty old man early."

"You hurt me with your accusation," he said. "Why not apologize with a kiss?"

So she bent over him and kissed him. Their tongues met, and her interest increased. She broke the kiss and kissed his chin and then his forehead. He pushed her shoulder with one finger, but she broke away to put the books on her night stand.

"Why don't you take off your nightgown too?" Ted asked before she could lie down. "It would be easier than sitting up again."

"What makes you think I need the nightgown off?" But she did take it off. "And why do you have your underpants on?" When he bared himself, he was only beginning to get erect.

With her lying on her back, he resumed the kiss. She reacted immediately. As he was trailing kisses, licks, and nibbles down her neck, she already felt her nipples firm and warmth spread through her belly. She needed something more from him, but she needed this slow progress even more.

When he did reach her breast, he did a thorough job of it. He kissed a circle around its base, and then a trail spiraling upward. As his mouth rose, slowly but inexorably, towards the nipple, her arousal rose with it. He went on to licking her areola while trying to avoid the nipple. Every time his tongue touched it, her breast felt hotter. He finally sucked it, but instead of sucking the heat out, it grew.

She had to restrain herself from grabbing his head to hold him there when he kissed a trail down to her cleavage. At least his chest hair was brushing her right breast while he did the spiral thing with her left breast. When he finally sucked that nipple, she did hold him in place. She rolled enough that her right breast was pressed against his chest, too.

"Roll over," he said when he had broken away from her grip.

"Ted, I'm ready now." Ready? She was practically dripping.

"But I'm not, really. I have only one shot left in me, and that was after resisting you last night. I should have met you when I was fifteen." And, she silently thought, when she was fifteen, too, and totally unready for sex, but she let him have his fantasy. "Youth is wasted on the young; at least, virility is."

When she rolled over face down, resting on her elbows, he kissed her seat before kissing a path up her spine. He was resting on one elbow himself, but he managed to get that hand under her left breast. The nipple throbbed between his two fingers.

The other hand stroked her labia from behind. When he rubbed them together, she felt her moisture run down between them. Even exposed to air almost everywhere, she was burning up. His kisses traveled up her spine, and she felt them scorch each vertebra. When his mouth scorched her neck, he thrust two fingers into her. They left a fever heat as they withdrew slowly. Then he was biting the back of her neck while stroking flames into her clit.

The fire flared, consuming her. She shuddered, and then fell on the bed. She kept shuddering as he kept stroking. Shortly after she could no longer respond, he removed his finger.

"There, dear," he said. "You were wonderful. You *are* wonderful." He was rubbing her back now. She rolled toward him. He backed up and then leaned down to kiss her forehead. She closed her eyes for his kisses to them, and that made his kiss to the bridge of her nose a surprise. She tried — and failed — to slow her breath for the real kiss, but he avoided her mouth. Despite their motion, he managed to kiss her breasts. He leaned far over to suck her left nipple. She couldn't take any more.

"No!" she said.

"Sure," he said. "There's plenty of time." He lay down beside her and pulled a sheet up. He hugged her under the sheet and occasionally kissed her shoulder. His cock, lying on her leg, felt thick and hot but still soft.

"You really want to spend the day making love?" she asked.

"Mostly making out. As I said, I'm not fifteen any more. The spirit is willing, even eager, but the flesh isn't up to more than twice today."

"And you figure that I am?" Making out, though, sounded great. She had enjoyed their early college years of kissing for the sake of kissing and stroking for the sake of stroking. The activity since had been goal-oriented. She loved the goal, but maybe she missed the kissing and cuddling for their own sakes.

"Hell, yes! Besides, one little part of you is warm and wet and snug. That's all I feel when I'm about to come. There is so much more of you which is delightful, too, and I need some time to appreciate it all." He raised up to kiss her eyebrow.

"You're a romantic." Like Ted-2011 had been.

"You're luscious," he said. "I'm just responding to you." He kissed her temple and then the top of her right ear. He spent a long time exploring her ear.

"That tickles," she said when he licked the center with his tongue. He moved to the lobe and sucked it. His teeth closed over it just short of hurting. When she shivered, he left her ear for her neck. He didn't use his teeth there, but he nibbled with his lips. That tickled, but he lay on her, pinning her so that her wiggles couldn't escape his mouth.

As his kisses went lower, he lifted himself off. After kissing up her right breast and sucking at that nipple, he kissed down to her cleavage. The trail went down her body, and the ticklishness resumed. He grabbed her elbows and rested his weight on them as he lapped at her navel.

"Ted."

"Busy," he said into her skin. He did leave her navel, but he kissed his way downward. When he blew through her pubic hair, that tickled in an entirely new way, and felt sexy as hell, too. His tugging some hairs up with his teeth felt sexy, and the idea of it was sexier yet. Then he sat back on his heels.

"Those bath salts smell better than they taste," he said.

"Well it was your idea, and you overdid them." Ted overdid most things.

He kissed the inside of her left thigh just above the knee. She felt the heat increase in her center as the kisses and licks approached it. She felt her muscles tighten as his tongue stroked the crease where her thigh met her vulva. Then he moved back to kiss her right thigh. The progression on this leg was probably the same as on the other one, but her arousal went higher. He kissed the labia, and then spread them with his thumbs.

"Ted!" She felt herself tense before his tongue touched her.

When he licked her labia, the tension spiraled up. Then his tongue touched her clit, and she went over. He kept on licking, though, and she kept on writhing. She grabbed his head, whether to hold him tighter or to push him away, she couldn't tell. Then he sucked her, and fire burned through her.

When she flopped down into the bed totally spent, he finally took his mouth from her. He moved up beside her and covered them both with the sheet. She felt one arm go around her, and that was all she felt for a while.

She came out of the doze certain that he was cuddling her lovingly even though only one arm was actually touching. She wasn't certain that she was awake yet, and his breathing sounded as though he were asleep, too. When she turned on her side and spooned back against him, though, he moved enough to pull the sheet from between them and adjust his hug to cup her left breast.

"Warm," she said. Her body was covered by the sheet where it wasn't wrapped in Ted.

"Ihm hmm." He squeezed the breast very lightly. He kissed the back of her head. She fell back asleep with his breath stirring her hair.

The radio jerked her awake. It was *Prairie Home Companion*. They tried to hear it every week, but she had unconsciously assumed that

Ted would treat his day of sex as more important. Instead, he'd reset the clock-radio for the start of the show.

As the show progressed, though, she understood his intention. Making out to Keilor was much better than making out to cartoons would have been. She turned so that they could have a nice kiss. When he scooted lower in the bed so that his face was level with her breasts, she decided to see how long he would content himself with them. He must have a limit, but she reached hers first. When the program got to Lake Woebegone, she moved down so that they were face to face. They kissed: sometimes deep, sometimes simply breathing each other, mostly gentle touches lip to lip.

When the show ended, Ted stretched to turn the radio off.

"We have to remember to reset the time," she said. Without the radio, they were certain to oversleep.

"Sunday." Ted was right. Oversleeping the next morning wouldn't make either one late for work. "Now . . ." He reached between her legs.

"Haven't we had enough foreplay?"

"That wasn't foreplay," he said, "just making out. Lie back." He began with light kisses over her face: cheek, ear, nose tip. She had been fairly aroused by the making out, and the kisses pushed her higher. When he progressed to deep kisses, his finger opened one set of lips while his tongue pierced the other.

As the heat spread from her groin, she became the aggressor. When her tongue chased his into his mouth, he sucked it. She grasped his cock, and it hardened in her hand.

"You," she said and spread her legs flat on the mattress.

"Yeah!" He got crawled between her legs. He spread her labia while she guided him between them. "Yesss." She raised her knees around him while he pressed into her. As deep as he could go, he wiggled on top of her until his hands clasped her breasts. He kissed her hairline.

Then he was taking deep, slow strokes, and the heat spread to her finger and toe tips. She felt herself clutch the sheets and push her pelvis up into his thrusts.

"Ted!" The flames licked her belly. She clutched around him and shuddered.

He drove into her and pressed her down. Through all her clasping and trembling, he was motionlessly rigid above her and in her. Every muscle in her body contracted once more, and then she collapsed.

When she was still, he began moving again. He moved higher in the bed over her, pulling her into a curve by the force of his cock. He stroked a fully rigid organ up and down into her in a beat even slower than before. There couldn't be anything left in her to arouse, but she began to react once more.

She curled her body and wrapped her legs around his hips. As the heat rose in her, she pulled him deeper into her with her legs on every stroke.

"Oh!" she said as she convulsed.

Ted rose up until he was barely in her. Then he drove down hard. "God!" he exclaimed. She could feel him pulsing within her contractions. He collapsed on her, his chest pressing on the left side of her face, and the pillow pressing on the right side.

She had one more spasm, and then she collapsed; her legs dropped down on the mattress. The last things that she noticed were that Ted was crushing her breasts and that he'd come out.

She awoke enough to notice that Ted was moving off her, and that it was easier to breathe. The next time she woke, the light in the room was from streetlights, not the sun. One of Ted's arms was across her, but he didn't touch anywhere else. She was sore in places that usually didn't get sore. Soon, though, she noticed that her bladder was full. She pushed the arm away and got to the bathroom.

When she was back in bed, he took his turn. They spooned and went back to sleep.

"Hungry?" he asked some unmeasurable time later.

"I'll fix something." Not quite yet, though. She tried to think what meal would use what they had and not take too much attention. She didn't think she was capable of attention right now. "How about spaghetti?" She had a jar of sauce.

"I'll get dressed and call out for pizza. You lie there and let it soak in."

"This 'soaking in' business had gone too far, Ted. This may be F day, but I'm probably not fertile now."

"You mean we'll have to do all this again next week?" He was trying his innocent look again. Practice hadn't made perfect.

The thought of this day's becoming another ritual suddenly horrified her. The first time they had made love in their new apartment had been a delight. The twentieth time he'd made love to her in the very same manner had been less delightful. If this elaborate process became a ritual, they would have nothing delightful left.

"Maybe not all of it," she suggested. "Maybe, a little of it. Maybe different pieces of it on different days."

She watched his thoughts chase one another across his face. Ted wasn't what you'd call sensitive, but he was intelligent — scarily intelligent, sometimes. He could tell she had — as softly as she could -- admitted that he repeated things too often. Then his face cleared.

"Variety? Do I choose the variety, or do you?" He'd asked a good question.

"Usually, you will." After all, she'd really enjoyed today. "Maybe, sometimes, I'll have a surprise for you." If she wanted variety in their marriage, she could put a little in. She was as willing to share that load as he was to share the other loads.

Surprise was the key. She would never warn him ahead of time. That meant that until he came through the door to find her wearing a sweat shirt and nothing else, he wouldn't know that this was about to be a special night. And that would mean that every time he came through the door he'd be wondering what she would be wearing. Sometimes, it might be just the necklace. (She'd turn down the air conditioner.)

She did love him more than yesterday, and if they both worked at it, she'd love him more tomorrow, too.

~~The End~~

Here is a sample from another story you may enjoy:

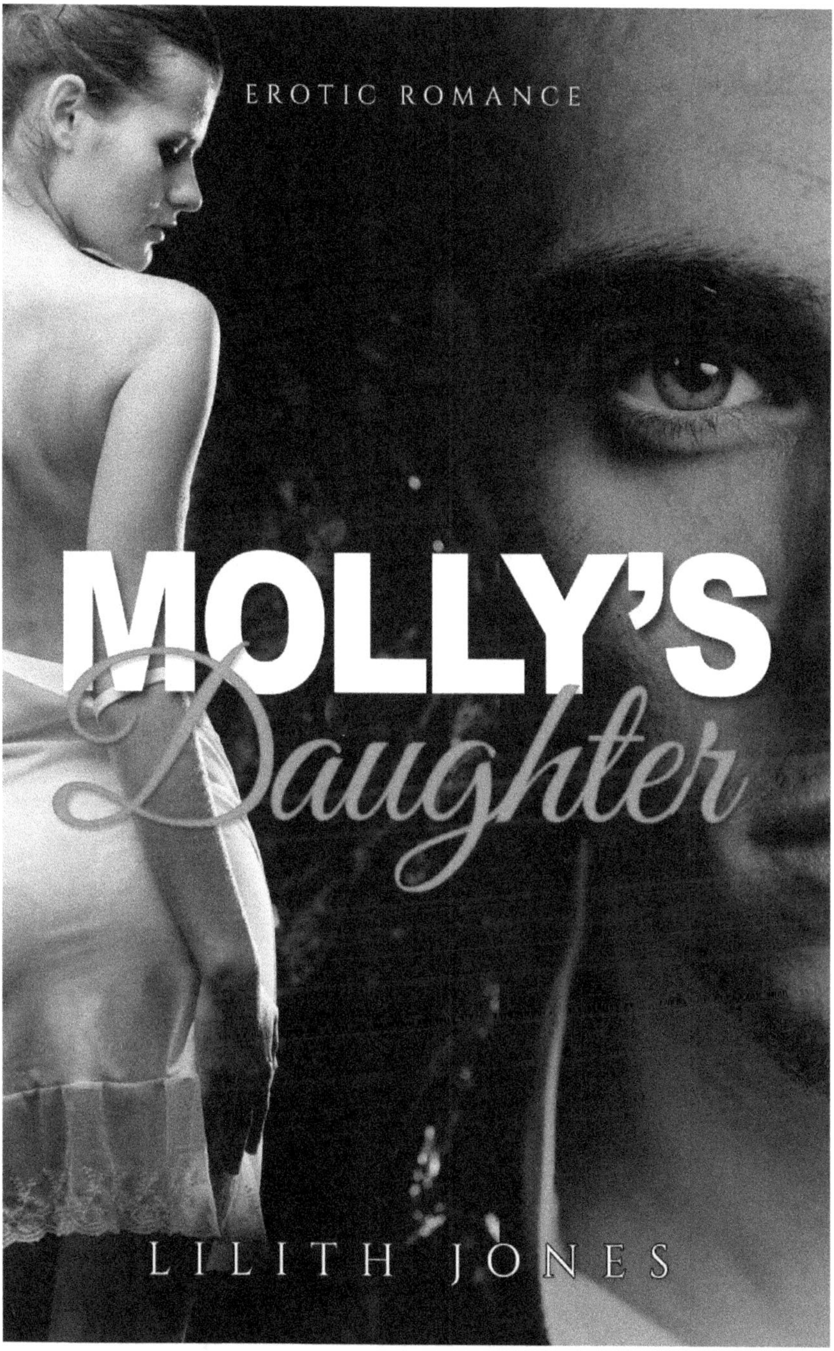
EROTIC ROMANCE
MOLLY'S
Daughter
LILITH JONES

After the lunch crowd had gone, Anne Bernard watched Mom from the window of the diner until she got to the house.

Minutes later, Mom called that she was lying down. Mom had handled the diner for years by herself. Anne hadn't appreciated how much work it was. Even when she had helped after school, she had bitched at how hard she worked instead of seeing the killing hours Mom had worked. And, then, she'd left Mom to handle it herself for three school years while she was in college. Mom had lied to her about the cancer when she was home for Christmas, though she could tell Mom wasn't feeling healthy.

Now, Mom still came in for lunch and dinner hours. It was Molly's Diner, and Molly still kept it up.

***

Greg Thibault shook the cell phone in his hand. He kept from throwing it across the mesa by telling himself that that would only make the situation worse. And a worse situation than the present would be unbearable. Every arrangement which had been "of course, Professor Thibault," or "no problem, Greg," when he had been in Boulder was unraveling at the other end of an unreliable connection.

"Look," he said, "I'll call you back in an hour or two with better reception." He punched off. He didn't know whether the guy at the department had heard him, but they would know that he wasn't on the line.

The phone companies boasted that they covered 99% of the people living in the country. This mesa was in the 1%. To be fair to the phone companies, not that Greg felt like being fair to any phone companies right then, the Anasazi weren't actually living in the United States. The last of them had been dead five centuries now.

He gave elaborate instructions to his students, descended by the footpath, and headed out in his Jeep. He took a quarter hour to get to something paved. The Jeep was supposed to be an off-the-road vehicle. It's just that the mesa was further off the road than the Jeep had been designed for. He found that his AC was dead, but he would have to climb back up the mesa and down again to get the keys for another vehicle. He opened the windows and got hot, moving air.

He wondered vaguely just why he'd bothered with giving the directions. Being a programming executive described as "like herding cats." Supervising archeological graduate students was like that, but worse. Everybody knew how to do the job better than the instructor did.

The nearest cellphone tower was between the two small towns of Randolph and Copper City. Randolph, the closer one, was more than an hour away. Even so, he passed only three cars on his way. Archeology got done in dry, empty country. It wasn't that Minnesota hadn't had cultures living in the area for millennia; it was that most of their artifacts had rotted or sunk into the ground. When the Anasazi had tossed out a potsherd, it was still where they'd tossed it.

He pulled into the parking lot of a diner in Randolph and called again. His hassles had only begun, and he spent half an hour on the cell, mostly on hold. By then, sweat was running down his body and pooling in the seat of his pants.

Hot, still air was worse than hot, moving air. And the air down here was, if anything, hotter than the air on the mesa. He looked across at Molly's Diner. He had seen the air conditioner when he'd driven in. His glasses were too streaked with his sweat now, but he could hear it when he listened. He'd been an idiot. He would go in and ask to make the other calls from there.

He'd left before lunch. He hadn't missed much. Assigning cooking duties only to coeds would be arrant sexism. On the other hand, guys who were going to major in Anthro didn't take home-ec in high school. Most girls who were going to major in

Anthro didn't take home-ec either. Or, if his present students had, they had forgotten everything they'd learned in that course.

The diner had an air conditioner. He could hear it. He'd eat and make the rest of his calls from there. He headed into the diner.

***

Anne didn't recognize the customer who came in. The non-local customers were truckers. How had an 18-wheeler got into the lot without her hearing it? The guy looked rugged, but not like a trucker, and she didn't know why for a minute. Then she did. He was tanned, deeply tanned, but the tone was even. Truckers had more tan on the left side.

She grabbed a menu, and the guy sat at the counter. She got behind the counter and handed him the menu. He took off his glasses and held the menu close.

"The home-made chile looks good," he said. "Might I have some of that?"

"Coffee?"

Greg shivered, and it wasn't the AC. That voice was the sexiest voice he'd ever heard. And she wasn't trying to be sexy. She had only asked if he wanted coffee.

"Please."

Anne poured him his coffee before getting the chile. Truckers, and many locals, were more interested in the coffee than in the food. She'd learned to brew good coffee. That meant pouring out a lot and alternating pots and scrubbing them often. A cup of coffee brought in more than making a pot cost, though, and truckers chose to stop based on the quality of the coffee.

Greg liked the coffee. The chile was the best-tasting food he'd had since he'd come to the mesa. Better than that, it tasted good. He got a napkin out of the dispenser and wiped off his glasses. The waitress was the sexiest woman he'd ever seen.

And it was neither her attitude nor her clothes.

She was wearing a blouse that covered her to the elbows and an apron over that. He'd spent the last two weeks with girls wearing shorts and halters, and none of them had been so attractive. The waitress had long hair, but it was tied up in a bun with a pencil stuck in it.

She hadn't presented the bill, but he paid with a $20. She brought him back his change. She stayed within sight while he ate, and that was easy on the eyes.

"Look, ma'am," he said, "the air is out in my Jeep. I have some calls to make from this area. I've been working in a dead zone." He held up his cell. "Would you mind if I made them from that table back there?"

Anne said, "Go right ahead. Want more coffee?"

"Please." This guy had said please more often to her in the last ten minutes than some regular customers had in the last month. She couldn't figure him. He didn't have a local accent. Something in his speech reminded her of the professors at Tempe, though they hadn't been that polite. He looked like he sweated every day in the sun, and he sounded like he spent his life in a library.

He stood at the counter until she had refilled his cup. Then he carried it to a table by the door. By the air conditioner, too, she noticed.

He talked on his cell. He'd been right that he had some calls to make. After the second, he drained his cup and put it down. She carried the pot to his table to refill the cup.

"You didn't have to do that," he said. "I could have gone back for it."

"I wait tables."

"And cook?"

"And sweep the place out at night," she said. "This place barely supports Mom and me. It couldn't pay for a big staff." How barely it supported them, she wasn't going to tell a stranger, however nice he talked.

"Well, I don't know about the sweeping, but if you cooked that chile, you did a damned fine job."

"Why, thank you."

A trucker came in for coffee and pie just then, and she didn't pay attention to the guy until the trucker was served. The guy got loud on the phone towards the end, though, and she could hear that. Apparently, he could tell.

"A lady can overhear me, which puts a real crimp in my vocabulary. But you can take the next down handbasket." The person at the other end apparently said something. "No. Both of you are women, but only one is a lady."

After he closed the cell, he brought his cup to the counter for more coffee and ordered a hamburger. He waited there for the burger, paid, and waited for his change. The driver went out and the guy went back to his table. He made another call and argued some more.

Greg was perfectly well aware that yelling on the phone didn't make them hear you any better. Sometimes, though, he couldn't resist. Finally, he ended his last conversation with Boulder and closed the cell. He brought his cup and saucer back to the counter.

"What sorts of pie do you have?"

Anne said, "Peach, apple, and cherry. We don't cook the pies, though." She couldn't figure why she'd said the last. Just that the guy had said nice things about the chile.

"I'll risk some cherry, anyway. And more coffee." She got the coffee and the pie. He paid immediately, using some of the change she'd given him earlier. She suddenly wondered whether the $20 bill was all the money he'd brought with him.

Greg ate the pie slowly. He told himself that he wanted to stay because of the coolness. The waitress was great to look at, and great to listen to, though she hardly spoke to him. Still, she was a pretty girl in a town full of young men. She was certain to be taken. He could look, but not touch.

"You were right," he said, pushing an empty plate and an empty cup away. "The pie was not home cooked. Nothing wrong with it, though. This is a nice place, how long are you open?"

That, he thought, was real suave, Thibault, not! 'When do you get off?' Indeed. The question isn't when she gets off, but where you get off.

"We're open six to ten."

"Thanks." He put a couple of bills under the edge of his plate and walked towards the door. "Really, thanks for everything," he said before going out. It would be a long drive back, and into the setting sun, too.

Anne said, "You're welcome," in a voice which was probably too low for him to hear. Then she got his dishes, spoon, and fork into the soaking water. There wouldn't be many customers before supper. She might as well wash the dishes now, so she did.

She put the tip into the cash register. About half the truckers and a quarter of the locals tipped. Their tips seldom folded. Of course, the guy had eaten a lot, and he had asked about making calls from here. But people called on cells from the diner all the time. Two free refills weren't a lot, and he sure hadn't made her walk. She did hear his car leave, though she hadn't heard it arrive.

Well, she'd tell Karen about the mysterious stranger in September, and she would invent one of her marvelous stories to explain him. Then Anne stopped smiling. Would she go back to school in September? Would she ever see Karen again?

If you enjoyed this sample then look for **Molly's Daughter**.

Also by this Author

About the Author

If you enjoyed any of my books then please share the love and promote my books in Amazon.

If you write me a review and send me an email I will send you a free book, or many.
(Just know that these emails are filtered by my publisher.)

Good news is always welcome.

One Last Thing, For Kindle Readers...

When you turn the page, Kindle will give you the opportunity to rate this book and share your thoughts on Facebook and Twitter. If you enjoyed my writings, would you please take a few seconds to let your friends know about it? Because... when they enjoy they will be grateful to you and so will I.

Thank You!

Lilith Jones
lilith_jones@awesomeauthors.org